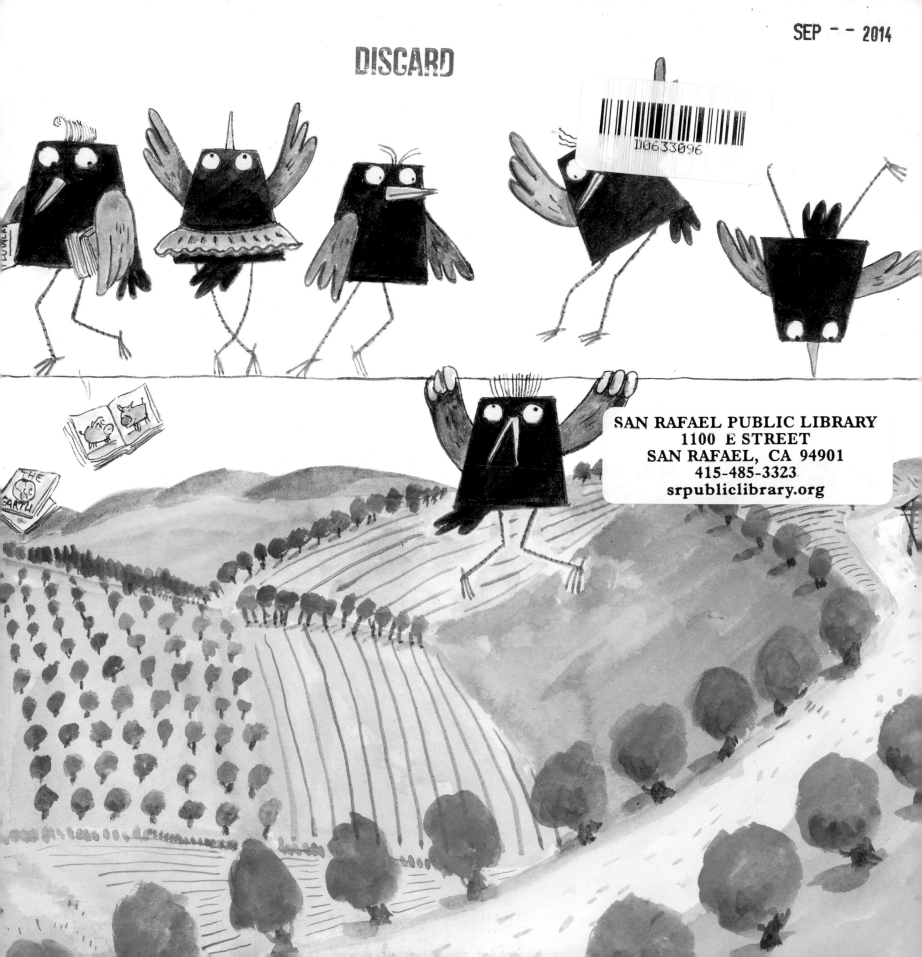

DISCARD

10633096

SAN RAFAEL PUBLIC LIBRARY
1100 E STREET
SAN RAFAEL, CA 94901
415-485-3323
srpubliclibrary.org

To Keith, Alli, and Caryn. Calvin loves you. —JB

For Betsy, whose love and support through the years has made this all possible. –KB

STERLING CHILDREN'S BOOKS
New York

An Imprint of Sterling Publishing
387 Park Avenue South
New York, NY 10016

STERLING CHILDREN'S BOOKS and the distinctive Sterling Children's Books logo are trademarks of Sterling Publishing Co., Inc.

Text © 2014 by Jennifer Berne
Illustrations © 2014 by Keith Bendis

All rights reserved. No part of this publication may be reproduced, stored in a retrieval system, or transmitted in any form or by any means (including electronic, mechanical, photocopying, recording, or otherwise) without prior written permission from the publisher.

Designed by Ellen Duda

ISBN 978-1-4549-0910-1

Library of Congress Cataloging-in-Publication Data

Berne, Jennifer.
    Calvin, look out! : a bookworm birdie gets glasses / by Jennifer Berne ; illustrations by Keith Bendis.
        pages cm
    Summary: Relates how Calvin the starling's book knowledge and new glasses aid him during a perilous adventure.
        ISBN 978-1-4549-0910-1
    [1. Starlings--Fiction. 2. Books and reading--Fiction. 3. Eyeglasses--Fiction.] I. Bendis, Keith, illustrator. II. Title.
    PZ7.B455143Cc 2014
    [E]--dc23
                                                                                    2013014444

Distributed in Canada by Sterling Publishing
c/o Canadian Manda Group, 165 Dufferin Street
Toronto, Ontario, Canada M6K 3H6
Distributed in the United Kingdom by GMC Distribution Services
Castle Place, 166 High Street, Lewes, East Sussex, England BN7 1XU
Distributed in Australia by Capricorn Link (Australia) Pty. Ltd.
P.O. Box 704, Windsor, NSW 2756, Australia

For information about custom editions, special sales, and premium and corporate purchases,
please contact Sterling Special Sales at 800-805-5489 or specialsales@sterlingpublishing.com.

Manufactured in China
Lot #:
2 4 6 8 10 9 7 5 3 1
04/14

www.sterlingpublishing.com/kids

Calvin, Look Out!

A Bookworm Birdie Gets Glasses

by Jennifer Berne
Illustrated by Keith Bendis

STERLING CHILDREN'S BOOKS
New York

SAN RAFAEL PUBLIC LIBRARY
1100 E STREET
SAN RAFAEL, CA 94901
415-485-3323
srpubliclibrary.org

Calvin curled up in his favorite corner of the library to read about dragons.

"Oops—that says 'WAGONS' not 'DRAGONS!'" He wondered, "Why is this book so blurry?"

Calvin decided to get another book, one he could see better.
"Here's one about a yellow dinosaur. Wait—that's not a dinosaur,
it's a chicken!"

Calvin turned to put the book back and tripped right over a chair.

"What's wrong with this library?!"

"Maybe it's your eyes, Calvin dear," said Mrs. Readalot, the librarian.

NEW BOOKS

RETURNS

"Perhaps you're farsighted. How many feathers am I holding up?"

Calvin focused very hard.

"Four? . . . Six? . . . Eight? Uh-oh, this calls for some research!

"Let's see . . . 'farsightedness'. . . trouble seeing near objects . . . blurry vision . . . it says 'Hy-per-o-pia.'

"Hyperopia! I have a horrible, rare disease! Oh, wait—it says it's common and simply remedied."

Calvin read that it's hereditary and wondered if that's why his Uncle Ralph used to walk into trees all the time.

"It says I need eyeglasses. Thanks, Mrs. Readalot."

So off went Calvin to Treeville to get himself some glasses.
"Let's see . . . a left and a right and . . . oh, here's the place!
Dr. Seewell, Optometrist."

After a little testing . . .

. . . fitting and adjusting . . .

. . . Calvin was on his way home wearing his beautiful new pair of SPECTACLES, as he preferred to call them.

He was so proud, he flew right over to show the flock.

"Calvin . . . what's that on your face?" Aubrey giggled.

"Hey, everybody, look at Calvin! He's got bug eyes!" Clement snickered.

"Jeepers creepers . . . Calvin's got new PEEPERS!" said Franklin as he started to guffaw.

Calvin's starling cousins laughed so hard they were falling off their branches! Calvin felt terrible.

"Oh," he sighed, "how your chirps of mockery lay heavy on my heart!"

Clement said, "Sorry Calvin, but you just look so . . . GEEKY!" And that got them laughing all over again.

Then Calvin remembered that
BEN FRANKLIN wore glasses.

And GANDHI.

And JOHN LENNON.

So he walked away, deciding he was in excellent company.

That's when Calvin realized he could see things he never saw before. Small things. Interesting things.

"Wow, I never knew moss was so beautiful!"

So he took his plant guidebook into the woods and went for a nature walk . . .
deeper and deeper into the woods.

Calvin was concentrating so closely on the little things, he didn't notice
that big rock balancing on those damp, mossy branches.

All of a sudden Calvin tripped. His foot
slipped, the branches snapped, the rock tumbled . . .
and there he landed, wedged between the rock and
a whole tangle of twigs.

"HORRORS, I'M STUCK!
What a perilous situation! I never should
have ventured so far into the woods alone!
I've got to stay calm and think."

But staying calm wasn't so easy, and a big tear rolled down his cheek.
"I'm too young to die! Was my whole life for naught?"

Through his tears, Calvin noticed the sun glinting off his eyeglasses. That reminded him of the story he read about Archimedes, the great Greek inventor. Calvin remembered how Archimedes used mirrors to reflect sunlight and set the attacking Roman ships on fire.

"Well," reasoned Calvin, "if his mirrors could reflect enough light to start a fire, I bet my spectacles could reflect enough light to send a signal."

So Calvin lifted his glasses and began to wiggle them back and forth, back and forth, catching the sun's light just right.

Flash-flash-flash. FLASH . . . FLASH . . . FLASH. Flash-flash-flash. Over and over again.

Back at home, Aubrey looked up and saw flickers of light coming from the woods.

"What's that?" she wondered.

Clement looked up. "It looks like some kind of signal."

Mr. Wingstead, their flight instructor, looked up too, and realized it was a signal for help.

"Three short flashes, three long flashes, three short flashes," he explained. "That spells S.O.S. in Morse code. Someone's in trouble!"

Off they all flew into the woods, guided by Calvin's flashes of light.

When the flock saw Calvin's terrible
situation they became extremely worried.
"Oh no . . . Calvin's trapped!"

"What do we do? We're so little, and that rock's so big!"
"Look at all those sticks. We'll never get him out of there!"

But Calvin had been stuck for a while, so he had done quite a lot of thinking.

"Get some vines—long ones. Tie them around the rock. Now get more and weave them around the sticks. Now all of you pull—really hard!"

They did exactly as Calvin instructed.
The whole flock pulled and tugged, and
tugged some more, until—with the biggest tug
of all—the rock went rolling away. The sticks
broke loose.

CALVIN WAS FREE!

That evening the whole flock gathered on the
treetop as Calvin retold—very dramatically—
the story of his perilous adventure.

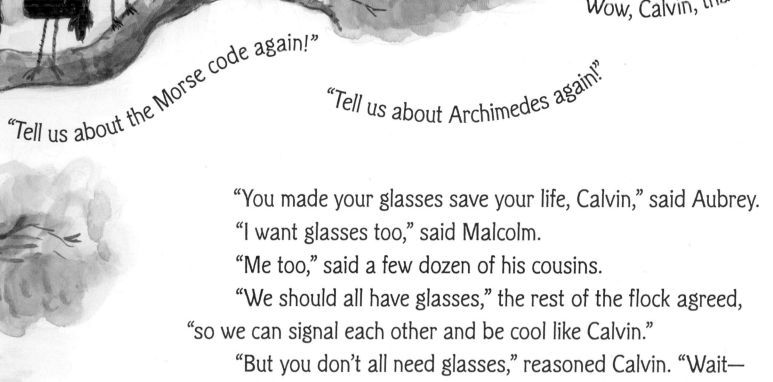

"Tell us about the Morse code again!"

"Tell us about Archimedes again!"

"Wow, Calvin, that's so cool!"

"You made your glasses save your life, Calvin," said Aubrey.

"I want glasses too," said Malcolm.

"Me too," said a few dozen of his cousins.

"We should all have glasses," the rest of the flock agreed, "so we can signal each other and be cool like Calvin."

"But you don't all need glasses," reasoned Calvin. "Wait— I have an idea! Get ready for a trip tomorrow."

The next morning they all flew into Treeville for a visit with
Dr. Seewell, who had a very busy day.

It turned out that 854 of Calvin's cousins had hyperopia and did need glasses. And the other 66,578 starlings got sunglasses—just in time to migrate.

So, as Calvin's family flew north for the summer,
they were the coolest flock in the whole, wide sky . . .
which made them all very happy and proud.

Especially CALVIN.